The Snoops

by Miriam Moss

illustrated by Delphine Durand

Dutton Children's Books
New York

The Snoops live

at number nine Keyhole Place.

They are the neighborhood busybodies

who pry and peek and nose out

everybody's secrets.

At a whiff of a whisper,

they prick up their ears,

hang on words,

drink in rumors.

At the hint of a **raised** voice, they are on their toes,

itching with interest, burning with curiosity.

The Snoops are all eyes.

They don't miss Michael Harries
Wiping off his mother's kiss,

Or the price tag

on Tilly Toddler's new shoes,

Or old Miss Spankie (who's lost her hankie),

wiping her nose on her sleeve.

They spy Mr. Cramp tipping buckets of snails over the fence...

...into LOCO LOUIE'S moonlit garden.

And then they watch LOCO LOUIE painting
Mr. Cramp's Cat.

They see the silent unscrewing of Mrs. McCafferty's gate

and watch it appear, newly painted, in Handy Andy's back garden.

as Miss McBride reverses into Mr. Hornsby's new car.

clatter

splinter

They hear drumming footsteps,

a whispering kiss,   the flick of a light,

the slam of a dOor —

THWUMP

then they spOt
Slippery Sam
Sliding off through
the bushes.

They hear
Doctor Blink's tires hissing flat
as Tricky Ricky flicks
his pocketknife closed
and saunters off.

They hear
the snagging tear
of Mr. James's pants
ripping on a drainpipe
after he's been locked out.

RRRIP!

The Snoops have sharp noses.

When **Dotty Miles's pig** disappears
they trace the smell of bacon cooking
back to **Hearty Harry's** kitchen.

They even **sniff out** which dog
did which **poop** where,
and plot it on a graph.

But...
The Snoops have One gigantic fear.
They are terrified of being snooped on themselves!

To keep their spirits up,
they sing a Snooping song
in low, trumpety voices.

Soon, everyone in Keyhole Place
gets fed up with being snooped on.
And, despite all their snooping,
the Snoops never guess.

So they don't find out about
the Secret meeting
in the café
round the corner.

They just watch
everyOne return in
dribs and drabs,
nudging each
other.

nodding knowingly toward number nine. This makes the Snoops nervous and unsettled.

So they snoop even harder.

They are so busy snooping that they don't even notice...